Ruthie
and the (Not So)
Teeny Tiny Lie

Laura Rankin

BLOOMSBURY
CHILDREN'S
BOOKS

Typeset in Buccardi
Art created with pencil and acrylic paints on watercolor paper
Book design by Donna Mark

Published by Bloomsbury U.S.A. Children's Books
175 Fifth Avenue, New York, NY 10010

Library of Congress Cataloging-in-Publication Data
Rankin, Laura.
Ruthie and the (not so) teeny tiny lie / by Laura Rankin. — 1st U.S. ed.
p.   cm.
Summary: Ruthie loves tiny things and when she finds a tiny camera
on the playground she is very happy, but after she lies and says
the camera belongs to her, nothing seems to go right.
ISBN-13: 978-1-59990-010-0 · ISBN-10: 1-59990-010-6
[1. Honesty—Fiction. 2. Behavior—Fiction. 3. Schools—Fiction.] I. Title.
PZ7.R16825Rut 2007   [E]—dc22   2006013192

First U.S. Edition 2007
Printed in China by South China Printing Company, Dongguan, Guangdong
5 7 9 10 8 6

All papers used by Bloomsbury U.S.A. are natural, recyclable products
made from wood grown in well-managed forests. The manufacturing processes
conform to the environmental regulations of the country of origin.

For all the wonderful teachers
who help our children through their
(not so) teeny tiny troubles

Ruthie loved tiny things—the tinier the better.
Her toys were the teeniest imaginable. She had dinky
dinosaurs, itty-bitty trains, ponies no bigger than your
pinky, and teddy bears that were barely there.

Ruthie loved finding tiny treasures too. At the beach she searched for the smallest seashells. The flowers she picked were no bigger than fairy wings. She even had an eggshell from a hummingbird.

And wherever Ruthie went, she carried
some teeny thing in her pocket.

One day at school recess, after jump rope and swings,
Ruthie took a turn on the twirling bar.

When she landed, she saw something in the grass.
It was a little box with a teensy window and an even
tinier button on top. She couldn't believe her luck.
It was a teeny tiny camera.

Ruthie looked through its little window. Then she pressed the button on top to take a picture. CLICK! Just like a real camera. This was absolutely the best thing Ruthie had ever found, and it was hers!

CLICK! CLICK! She tried it out every which way.

"Say cheese, clouds." CLICK!

"Say cheese, little bug." CLICK!   "Say cheese, school." CLICK!

"Say cheese, Martin." CLICK!
But Martin didn't say "cheese." Martin said,
"Hey, that's my camera!"

Ruthie was startled. "No it's not, it's mine."
"Give it to me," said Martin. "It's mine!"
"It is not!"
"Is too!"

"No it's NOT!" shouted Ruthie, and she raced back to class.

"What's going on?" asked Mrs. Olsen.
"Ruthie's got MY camera!" cried Martin. "I got it
for my birthday and I dropped it on the playground."

But Ruthie wanted that teeny tiny camera in the worst way.
"It's mine!" she yelled. "I got it for MY birthday!"
Well, that wasn't true at all. Not one teeny tiny bit.

Mrs. Olsen looked at Martin. She looked at Ruthie. "Goodness, this *is* a problem," she said. "The camera can't belong to both of you. I'll keep it safe in my desk drawer for now. Let's talk about it again tomorrow."

Ruthie's stomach flip-flopped
all the rest of the day.

She couldn't remember
the answer to 2 + 2.

When Mrs. Olsen read
a story, every word flew
straight out the window.

The bus ride home took forever.

"Hi, Ruthie," said Momma. "How was school?"
"Okay," mumbled Ruthie.

Dinner was macaroni and cheese, Ruthie's
favorite, but she couldn't eat. Not one little bite.
"Aren't you feeling well?" asked Papa.
"I'm not hungry," she said.

At bedtime, Ruthie was close to tears.

"What's the matter?" asked Momma.

So Ruthie told Momma and Papa the whole story.

"What do you think went wrong?" asked Papa.

"I said it was my camera," cried Ruthie, "but it's not!"

"It's going to be okay," said Papa. "You made a mistake, and tomorrow you can fix it. I think Mrs. Olsen and Martin will understand."

But the next morning, Ruthie could barely eat. Maybe Mrs. Olsen wouldn't understand. Maybe Ruthie would have to sit in the time-out corner. Maybe Martin would never talk to her again. Maybe *no one* would ever talk to her again . . . not one teeny-weeny word.

The school bell was about to ring.
Ruthie took a deep breath and began
the long walk to the front of the room.
Mrs. Olsen's desk seemed very far away.

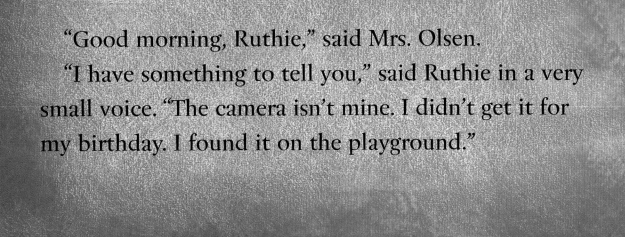

"Good morning, Ruthie," said Mrs. Olsen.

"I have something to tell you," said Ruthie in a very small voice. "The camera isn't mine. I didn't get it for my birthday. I found it on the playground."

Mrs. Olsen didn't make her sit in the time-out corner. She didn't even look mad.

Instead, she gave Ruthie a hug and kissed the top of her head. "Thank you for telling the truth," said Mrs. Olsen. "That took a lot of courage."

"I'm very sorry, Martin," said Ruthie.
"It's okay," said Martin.

All at once, Ruthie's stomach stopped flip-flopping. She even skipped a little on the way back to her desk.

She got the right answer to 3 + 7 in math.

After lunch, Mrs. Olsen read the funniest story
Ruthie had ever heard.

And on the short bus ride home, Ruthie realized she didn't miss the teeny tiny camera . . . not one teeny tiny bit.